My
Fairytale 2

—A ROMANTIC DRAMA SEQUEL—

Raquel McFarland

ISBN: 979-8-9918295-2-6 (Print)
ISBN: 979-8-9918295-3-3 (E-book)

Printed in the USA

DEDICATION:

This is dedicated to those who provide daily inspiration and support. Because of you, I am able to be me. Thank you for all you do.

Second Book, Done!!!

TABLE OF CONTENTS

FOREWORD

She's back at it again! After reading the debut, you were left asking 'When is the next book coming out?' and demanding 'I need to know what is going to happen next!' Well, the wait is finally over!

In this sequel, Raquel McFarland leaves you with many cliffhangers that lead up to an unexpected end. New players have been introduced, some of whom have shady dealings. Once again, what you think is about to happen next, isn't what occurs.

Get ready to be glued to your seat as you weave your way through all of the twists and turns. This sequel is sure to leave you wanting more.

Kiara Roberts

MARITAL BLISS

"Welcome home Love!" KB cooed as he carried Alexis over the threshold.

They had just returned from their two-week long honeymoon in Bora Bora. It was a beautiful time in a beautiful place with crystal clear water, calm, serenity. Walking along the beach, snorkeling, sailing…so much fun and relaxation. This was a much-needed break for both of them. They enjoyed each other thoroughly, having the most fun feeding each other fresh fruit and sipping on drinks while sitting at the edge of the water.

"So glad I waited for Mr. Right! KB is definitely it! My dad is definitely looking out for me up above. Thank you, God, for answering my prayers!!" Alexis was quietly saying to herself while staring at KB with adoration.

"Dear?!" KB says with impatience. "This woman is always drifting off into her own world." KB thinks to himself. He wished she would let him in more but doesn't push the issue. Part of him will always be concerned about how they came to be and if that has any impact on their future, even though she said yes and still married him.

"Huh?" Alexis says as she is shaken out of her thoughts. "There he goes with that word again…. at least this time I'm okay with him saying it." She says to herself.

"Yes, Dear!" Alexis shoots back with the same impatience in her voice and rolling her eyes at the same time. He threatens to throw her on the couch but thinks better of it. He didn't want to be sleeping alone on that same couch on their first night home.

They laugh as KB continues to carry Alexis into the living area of their home. He spins her around in circles, making them both dizzy. Planting a big kiss on her lips as they come to a stop, they erupt into laughter again.

"Whoo, you getting a little heavy." KB jokes as he proceeds to put her down. To add to the dramatics, he is breathing extra hard. He bends over with his hand on his chest and the other on his hip. "I gotta catch my breath!" He jokingly says, much to her dismay.

"Oh, I see you got jokes!" she responds while rolling her eyes.

"What? It is not my fault you ate everything put in front of you and me! I mean, the shrimp had no luck with you around. You ate so much chocolate, they ran out. They had to ship in more grapes to make the Moscato because you drank it all..." KB goes on and on.

Alexis drifts off into her own thoughts again, ignoring KB's criticisms of her eating habits. "This is the most wonderfulest thing that has ever happened to me. I am so happy, the happiest I could ever be. Who would have thought I would be married to the finest most bestest man in the whole ENTIRE world!" All of a sudden in the background she hears music...interrupting her thoughts.

"Aw yeah! That's my jam!" KB shouts and grabs Alexis by the hand. He spins her around and wraps his arm around her waist. Pulling her close to him, they begin to sway back and forth. He rests his forehead on hers. They close their eyes...then the moment is ruined as he begins to sing along.

She laughs and joins him. They laugh and sing and dance for the next half hour.

"I'm getting hungry…" Alexis begins until KB cuts her off.

"When are you not hungry? If I had known you could eat so much, I might have kept it moving. Now, get in there and cook us something to eat before I pass out."

Before KB could start the next sentence, a pillow from the couch landed upside his head. Alexis crossed her arms and rolled her eyes while standing like she had much attitude and tapping her fingers on her arm. As she peeks out of the corner of her eye, she sees KB running toward her. She took off running and locked herself in the bedroom.

"I got you right where I want you." KB says with a big cheesy grin on his face. He pretended to walk away, listening for Alexis to unlock the door. Click. She fell for it. He barges into the room, grabs her, and lifts her over his head. In one smooth move, he gently throws her on the bed, jumps on top of her and begins tickling her. They soon forget about being hungry.

A sudden knock at the door interrupts their deep passionate kisses, just as things began to heat up between them.

"Who could that be? We just got home!" KB says with disappointment and frustration at the interruption. He grabs his t-shirt from the floor and quickly pulls it over his head. Then he picks up his gun belt from the night stand beside the bed and puts it on, checking to make sure his gun was ready.

"All I know is, it better not be those durn kids from down the street! It's like they can sniff out when we are at home or something." Alexis says as she is huffing and puffing, struggling to get up from the bed and buttoning her shirt. Those extra pounds she put on were weighing her down and had her thinking about her weight loss plan she needed to start immediately.

As they make their way to the door, a sudden strange feeling comes over Alexis. KB gently pushes the curtain to the side and carefully looks through the blind to see who might be outside. His other hand on the gun on his waist. Alexis looks through the peephole which was made of bulletproof glass, an added feature her dad had installed for protection when the house was built.

"Hmmm, no one." She says and proceeds to review the footage from the cameras KB strategically placed around the outside of their home before leaving on their honeymoon. Still seeing no one, Alexis slowly opens the door and looks left to right, right to left. No one in sight. Looking down, she sees that there is a small box on the welcome mat with a white bow on top and a note that says "Congratulations."

Waiting to Make a Move

"She thinks she is all that!" Bonquisha rants and raves as she paces in her living room. A hole was beginning to form in the rug due to all the pacing. The more she thought about it all, the more upset Bonquisha became.

"How could she do this to me? That is a straight up traitor move!" She yells to the walls that are listening since no one else was there. "I mean, I know dude is fine and all, but come on, there are others out there! She could get another one…I know I played a part in introducing them but you can't blame me! If it wasn't for me, she would still be stuck in la la land wishing she had someone…"

Bonquisha plops down on the couch and grabs the remote like it owed her something. She turns on the TV and flips through the channels stopping on the news. After about five minutes, she turns off the TV and throws the remote across the room causing the back cover to pop off and the batteries to fall out as it lands on the floor by the wall.

"I gotta get out of here! These walls are caving in on me and I can't breathe!" Bonquisha says to herself as she goes into the bedroom to change clothes.

After getting dressed, in all black of course, she hops in her car for a drive. First stop is the convenience store, gas and snacks are a must. She pumps gas and then proceeds into the store to buy some snacks. The clerk is eyeing her like she stole something as soon as she walked in or he wanted her, one or the other. Either way Bonquisha was not in the mood for foolishness. She sucks her teeth as she is walking up and down each aisle in the store on purpose to make the clerk even more nervous of her presence. Smacking on gum loudly and blowing huge bubbles to add to the dramatics, she grabs different items and then puts them back.

She finally decides on the snacks she wants, barbecue chips, chocolate chip cookies, honey roasted peanuts, strawberry blow pop, and grape bubble gum. With her hands full, she grabs a bottle of water along with an energy drink. As she heads to the counter, she spots a honey bun and wiggles her way down to grab it and add it to her collection, careful not to drop anything. The clerk is still eyeing her, almost making it to where she wants to drop everything on the floor right where she stood and walk out. Instead, she proceeds to place everything on the counter to be rung up as she is going to need those snacks to keep her company.

The clerk is ringing up her items and she decides to buy a lottery ticket and two scratch offs as well. He seems annoyed that she added more items. After ringing up everything, he flashes a big smile while telling her the total and asking her if she wants a bag. "No he didn't!" She says to herself in response to his fake smile.

After paying for her items, she grabs the bag and as she is walking out, she turns and gives the clerk a wink. Laughing all the way to her car, she doesn't see the van that pulls into the parking lot and nearly misses hitting her. Her mood instantly changes and she begins to bless the driver with a few choice words and finger gestures. The driver returns the same.

Getting into her car, she checks the mirror to make sure her hat is still on tight and the ponytail is hanging out of the back just right. Then she situates the snacks and drinks so they can be accessed easily while driving. A quick check of her phone for any messages. None. Logging into the tracker account on her phone, Bonquisha confirms the location of Alexis. She and Alexis had set this up a long time ago so they would always know where each other was at all times in case one or the other was in trouble and needed help. Alexis must have forgotten about it and until she did, Bonquisha was going to continue to use it.

"Alright, here we go." Bonquisha says while driving down the road to where Alexis was unsuspectingly minding her business. She arrives after what seemed like an hour of driving, finds a parking space close to the doors for a speedy getaway, and gets out. Entering the store, she looks around and spots Alexis, making sure not to be seen. Bonquisha made it her mission to track Alexis' every move daily.

"I got something for her. She will not see me coming." Bonquisha was waiting for the right time to make a move. She needed the help of Pookie and his goons but wasn't sure she could wait for Pookie to get out. His homie, Ant (short for Ant'tony), kept trying to reach out to her every so often. And speak of the devil, her phone rings interrupting her surveillance and thoughts…

"What!?!" Bonquisha answers with a hint of annoyance in her tone. She almost forgot she was tailing Alexis and had to lower her voice to a whisper to avoid being heard. She peered around the pillar to make sure of Alexis' location and that she didn't hear her screaming at Ant.

"Hold up, Shorty! It ain't gotta be like dat!" Ant says while laughing to ease the tension. He knew Bonquisha didn't like him. She would never speak to him when he was around and she did everything she could to avoid him.

"Shorty?! Last I checked you are the short one!" Bonquisha replies. "Now whatchu' want? I'm busy!" She continues in an uncaring tone and laughs to herself thinking about his full name. Who names their child 'Ant'tony'? What were they thinking, or not thinking? Were they high? All these questions came into her head while Ant was going on and on about nothing she wanted to hear. She had this strange feeling he was up to something and she wasn't too far off from the truth. Her instincts were never wrong, well, until KB came around. Thinking about KB really enraged her so much that she hung up on Ant in order to finish her surveillance of Alexis.

Ant was left looking at the phone and thinking "What just happened?".

PRISON TALKS

"What up, tho!" Pookie says through the phone after his homie Ant accepts the collect call from prison. "I been on this good behavior kick, really hoping to get out sooner than later."

"Oh yeah? That's what's up!" Ant responds.

"You been in touch with Bonquisha?" Pookie asks.

"Yeah, man. She HOT." Ant says with emphasis.

"I know she is. She finally landed that fool of a cousin of mine only to lose him. I know she glad she has that rock tho'." Pookie responds.

"Whoo, man, did you see it?" Ant inquires.

"Yeah, I was with him when he picked it up. That mug is blinging for real! I tried to talk him out of it. I kept saying, man, don't buy no 3-carat diamond ring for her. He cut me off before I could even finish my sentence. He was serious 'bout her!" Pookie remembers as he carelessly tells Ant the size of the diamond.

"Hhmmm..." Ant makes the sound as he is now focused on how he can get his hands on it. That would be a huge come up for him.

"What you say?" Pookie asks

"Huh? Oh, nuthin'!" he responds.

"But mannnn, look here. I only have a couple mo' minutes on this phone. Get with Bonquisha and find out what she thinking. Hit me back tomorrow." Pookie instructs and then the phone cuts off.

"Again?! Twice in the same week! I'm not going to keep getting hung up on! One more time, one more time...." Ant shouts, then catches himself as he realizes this time doesn't count. What was more embarrassing was that no one was around to hear him make these threats. He had to laugh at himself.

"Dang, these phone privileges got to get better!" Pookie says more to himself but loud enough that others could hear him. He begins to think of who on the inside can get him a phone to use. Then he hears some commotion coming from down the hall. As he is heading back to his cell, he looks around the corner to see who is involved in the brawl. Pookie shakes his head… "Same ol' guys doing the same ol' thang, day in and day out! I'm trying to get out. Forget what they trying to do. This ain't fo' me! I'm too pretty fo' dis!"

His cellmate could hear him talking to himself and was laughing hysterically. "Man, you always talkin' to yourself!" he continued to laugh.

Pookie gave him a look, the look, and he immediately shut up. He knew who Pookie was and knew his cousin too. With Raheim gone, Pookie is the head guy now and that title came with much respect, and responsibility. Was Pookie ready for all of the responsibility? Only time will tell but he had to act the part or else be eliminated and he couldn't let that happen. He had to honor his cousin's name and reputation.

Broken out of his thoughts by the sound of a baton banging against the bars, Pookie looks up to see the night shift officer. She had this big grin on her face like she was happy to see him. Knowing who he was excited her and she wanted him to know it. Every day at the beginning of her shift, she made it a point to stop by and visit him. This is the person that is going to bring him a phone he thought as he returned the smile, showing all of his teeth.

"You doing alright today?" she asked.

"I'm much better now that you are here." Pookie replies, trying to be smooth as he leans against the bars and looks her up and down. He was flirting real hard so she would be more willing to get him what he wanted.

"You need anything?" she says, while sucking her teeth thinking about what she could get from him.

"Now that you mention it, I could use your help getting something in particular." He states.

"What's that? Whatchu need honey?" she inquires.

He puts his hand to his ear in such a manner as to suggest a phone and nods his head. Then flashes a big smile and winks at the officer to add extra effect in his efforts to convince her to oblige. Really piling it on, he flexes his muscles and gives what he thinks is a sexy mean mug. Inside, he is laughing hysterically because he knows she is not his type. Hey, whatever it takes, he reasons with himself.

"I gotchu!" she replies and winks.

As she walks away, Pookie, thinks about his plans when he gets out. First, he has to reestablish his living arrangements and then get his ride. Fortunately, he was smart enough to stash some cash at his mom's house. He bought her a house in the country, just far enough to keep her from being found and close enough to get to her when he needed.

An hour had passed and it was now time for dinner. "Man, don't nobody want this nasty slop." Pookie utters under his breath. In order to eat, he had to imagine he was enjoying his mother's home cooking. That was the only way he could stomach it. With each bite, he envisions roast beef with gravy, mashed potatoes, greens, and sweet cornbread.

Finally finishing his dinner, if that's what you want to call it, Pookie heads to his cell. He notices a package on his bed and begins to smile. Thinking "oh, she delivered!" while trying to open the package, disappointment soon settles in as he realizes it is not what he was hoping it would be. He throws the package down on the bed and then washes his hands in the sink.

Ready to get some shut eye, he lays down placing his hands behind his head. While getting comfortable, he feels some strange object under his pillow. Reaching underneath, he touches the object with his fingertips. A big cheesy grin comes over his face and his heart began to pound, beating faster than normal. He almost could not contain his excitement.

SETTLING IN

"Finally!" Alexis shouted!

"What?!?" KB returned with a crazed look on his face.

"We finally got all your stuff moved in and incorporated. You had a lot of stuff! How does one accumulate so much? Geez!" Alexis rambled on while KB rolled his eyes.

"You can't talk my dear! There is an entire closet in the guest room full of clothes with tags on it that I have not and will never see you wear!" KB replied.

They both looked at each other and started laughing. KB ran over to Alexis and grabbed her by the waist. He pretended like he was going to kiss her and then threw her on the bed. As he jumped on top of her to begin tickling her, Alexis pounded him in the face with a pillow. They always played this way, like two little kids or something.

"Oh, it's like that?? Bet!" KB rolled over and dropped to the floor. He reached under the bed for the water gun he had stashed while Alexis wasn't looking. Staying ready, so he thought!

"Yep! It's like that!" Alexis shouted while giggling. Unbeknownst to KB, she was already in the bathroom pulling out her super soaker water gun from under the sink. Always ready, that's what her daddy taught her.

KB pops up and begins spraying the water gun in the direction of Alexis. Screaming like in a war zone, Alexis pulls the trigger on her water gun. She is walking towards KB while spraying him. He acts like the force of the water is pushing him over so that he falls to the floor. Alexis stands over him and asks if he is ready to surrender. He responds "Never!" then crosses his arms and puts his hands over his face.

"OK, I gave you a chance." Alexis replies and empties all the water out of her super soaker onto KB, laughing hysterically. "Take that!" she continues. Before she knew it, KB jumped up, grabbed her by the waist, almost like a football tackle and threw her onto the bed again.

"Back where we started!" KB retorts with a sneaky smile.

"Stop! Stop!" Alexis screams between laughs. "We have to finish unpacking ALLLLLL of your things. Stop!" She pleads to no avail. KB is tickling her and this time it is worse because they are both soaking wet, KB more than Alexis.

After about five minutes, Alexis is able to put KB in a chokehold with her legs and flip him off of her onto the other side of the bed. She darts up and runs into the bathroom, locking the door behind herself. Unable to stop laughing the entire time, she bends over holding her stomach and breathing hard.

"I see you are putting the techniques I taught you to use." KB says while getting up from the bed to begin straightening up the mess they made.

While in the bathroom, Alexis drifts into her fairytale world, imagining the next phase of her life and feeling elated about how it has turned out so far. The man of her dreams in the house of her dreams living the life of her dreams, what more could she ask for…what more?

Snapping out of her thoughts, she hops in the shower. After getting dressed, she proceeds to help KB with cleaning up, although he is almost done. Perfect timing! Seeing he is almost finished; she ventures into the kitchen to make a snack. All that playing around made her hungry and she was sure he was hungry too.

"Honey, what do you want to eat?" Alexis yells from the kitchen.

"Whatever you make is fine." KB shouts back.

"I don't think we have any 'whatever you make is fine' in the refrigerator!" she says slyly. "You better tell me what you want or you won't be eating." she continues as she grabs an apple for herself. Rinsing and drying it, she takes a big bite and juices from the apple fly all over the place.

"What did that apple do to you?" KB startles Alexis, appearing in the kitchen with his shirt off and showing all of his muscles.

"Shut up!" Alexis replies with a frown on her face. She was trying her best not to laugh but couldn't help herself. "Want a bite?" she asks.

"No, no! You got that one. I'll get my own." he returns jokingly while grabbing one from the bowl on the counter. Then, he thinks about the banana and ponders getting that instead. Ultimately, he decides on the apple as originally planned.

As he is eating the apple, he is watching Alexis do her thing in the kitchen. One of the reasons he married her was because of her delectable dishes. She really knew how to cook and he thoroughly enjoyed watching her. It was like she was in another world and by the time she finished, not only was the food good, the plating of it was stellar and the kitchen was clean. "I picked the right one!" he whispers to himself.

"What you say?" Alexis asks, not missing a beat nor turning away from the food.

"What are you over there cooking? It smells delicious!" KB responds, embarrassed that she almost heard him openly speak his thoughts. While she is putting the finishing touches on the plating of the food and explaining what she had cooked, KB gets a bottle of wine from the fridge and two wine glasses.

"Table or living room?" he asks, patiently waiting on her response.

"Table, my Dear." Alexis says with a smile knowing she was mocking him calling her 'Dear' all the time.

She is grabbing the plates and walking toward the table. KB sets the wine and glasses down and doubles back to get forks and napkins. They really enjoyed sitting at the table together, staring into each other's eyes. The scenery outside of the window added to the romantic flair of the moment. They sit in silence, savoring the tenderly cooked salmon, asparagus, almond wild grain rice pilaf, and lightly buttered crispy croissants.

IN THE SHADOWS

While out shopping, that strange feeling came over Alexis again. She shrugged it off and kept looking for that perfect outfit. KB had planned a special night for her and she needed to make sure she was on point. This was especially difficult because she didn't have her used to be best friend with her to help pick out something fly and sexy but elegant. The thought made her a bit sad, but only for a hot second.

"Hmph! She gets to enjoy life! Go on shopping sprees! Be happy! It's not right! It's not right!" Bonquisha thought to herself as she followed Alexis around the mall. This was actually quite fun for Bonquisha, better than sitting around in the house staring at the walls, staring at the beautiful ring Raheim had given her and talking to herself. The ring hadn't come off of her hand since the day he put it on her finger and she didn't plan on ever taking it off.

Alexis moved about the mall, pausing every so often as she couldn't shake that strange feeling. It was becoming more and more frequent. Maybe she was just paranoid, for no reason. Little did she know, Bonquisha was just on the other side of the pillar, hiding in the shadows and laughing to herself.

This was the only 'fun' Bonquisha could muster although it was somewhat nerve wrecking. It all seemed like a waste of time but it helped to pass the time. The exact moment to put her plan, whatever it is, into action would be determined by all of this surveillance. Alexis' schedule changed since they used to hang out which is why this was necessary.

Alexis finished shopping for what she thought would be the best outfit for the special night ahead. For a minute she became nervous as she thought she saw Bonquisha. False alarm. It was someone else that had the same mannerisms. "Nahhh, that couldn't be. She would come up to me, right?" Alexis thought to herself as she continued to leave the store.

Bonquisha quickly ran and ducked behind the rack of clothes, pretending like she dropped something. She leaned over to pick up the imaginary item from the floor. It was too soon to have a run in with Alexis at this point. More time was needed to concoct the perfect plan. Surveillance needed to continue just a bit longer. Once the coast was clear and Alexis had left out of the store, Bonquisha slowly came from behind the rack of clothes.

"Wooh, that was too close! I gots ta' be mo' careful! Too slick to get caught. Stealth like a cat." Bonquisha uttered to herself. People around her in the store were staring at her like she was crazy. She began to think she was crazy for doing this but she had to avenge her beloved Raheim.

Standing inside the door, Bonquisha watched as Alexis drove off. "I guess that is enough surveillance for now. I need some real food! Those snacks done wore off. Hmmm, I bet Ant would love to take me out to eat." Bonquisha pondered the thought of going out to eat with Ant. Could she stomach it? She only considered it because she didn't want to spend her own money.

The call was made, reluctantly, and the 'date' was set. Ant arrived promptly at seven o'clock to pick up Bonquisha. Little did she know he had ulterior motives. Ant knocks on the door and the first thing she sees is a big bouquet of flowers. He hands the flowers to her, flipping his wrist in the process to show off his gigantic gold watch with diamonds around the dial. It was fake, but he was hoping she wouldn't notice.

"Awww, how nice!" Bonquisha forces herself to say as she takes the flowers and laughs to herself at his efforts to show off his fake watch. She leaves him standing at the door while she walks away to put the flowers in water. He doesn't mind because he gets to watch her walk away and also survey the surroundings. She returns and catches him looking around.

"Whatchu lookin' around fo'!?" she says angrily while closing the door behind her and locking it. This almost cost him the 'date' as she really didn't want to go with him in the first place. "Let's go!" she yells at him and rolls her eyes.

Standing by the car door waiting for him to open it and sucking her teeth at the same time, he realizes his second mistake. He runs over to the other side of the car. "Hold on Shorty, here I come." he says to her, almost too late as she had started to walk back toward her door.

"Look, I have certain expectations. If you gon' be takin' me out, you got to come right! An' DON'T be reading into nuthin'! I'm just hungry and didn't feel like cooking. Now drive!" Bonquisha lays down the law to Ant so he understood.

They rode in silence to the restaurant. She had provided the address and made reservations ahead of time. A table in the back where they couldn't be seen was required. One because she didn't want to be seen with him, and two because she didn't want Alexis to see her. It was risky, but Bonquisha had to be there. Ant had no idea he was on a surveillance mission.

Right on time, Alexis and KB arrived at eight o'clock. Their table was midway across the restaurant. Bonquisha was able to watch their every move and thankful she overheard Alexis on the phone while at the store so she would know where to be and when. Ant was seated with his back toward them so he was oblivious to what Bonquisha was doing. After every bite of food, she looked over at their table taking mental notes. When Alexis got up to go to the restroom, Bonquisha was able to see her outfit.

"What the H-E-Double Hockey Sticks?" Bonquisha blurted out just loud enough for Ant to hear her.

"What?!" Ant responds to her outburst.

"Oh, nuthin'! I just thought I saw something." she recovers.

"How's your food?" Ant tries to make conversation.

"It's fine." she replies. She had no interest in small talk. It was already awkward and she didn't really want to be there with him. But, to make sure he paid, she tried to show a little more interest in what he had to say. As usual, he wasn't really talking about much, however, she did notice that he kept looking at her hands and commenting on how nice they looked with her nails done and all. "Weirdo! I've heard of a foot fetish but a hand fetish?" she thought to herself.

GETTING OUT

The sound of a gavel banging is heard as people are gathering in the court room. There was quite a crowd as there were many cases to be heard. The main attraction was that of Pookie and members from the media did all they could to sneak in and get the exclusive. Some posed as regular attendees and dressed down to avoid being recognized. The judge knew a few of them personally and had them removed after recognizing them. They were prepared with an intern the judge didn't know so they could still get the story.

The gavel bangs again. "Raymond Clarence Smith, III, please step forward." The judge commands Pookie.

"Yes, your Honor." Pookie replies, embarrassed that she called his full name. No one ever knew what it was besides his cousin Raheim. While walking forward, he took a quick look back to make sure his goons were not laughing. Of course, Ant had a big cheesy grin which sealed up as soon as he saw Pookie look at him. Now he can start thinking about what name he is going to go by when he gets out.

"Are you aware of why you are here today?" The judge asks.

"Yes, your Honor." He replies.

His lawyer was late as usual and he gave her the side eye. She was fumbling through papers while the judge was talking. The judge had to stop and ask if she was ready or needed more time to which she replied she was ready. It didn't look like it though. Pookie was already considering getting another lawyer and upset at Ant for connecting him with this lady as she obviously didn't know what she was doing.

Pookie had filed an appeal to get his sentence reduced. Time was of the essence and he needed to get back out there to keep things going. Trusting his homies to take care of things was not something he could afford to do. His cousin Raheim taught him that. Grandma taught him that if he wanted something done right, he had to do it himself. It was crucial for him to get out sooner than later. There was only so much he could do from behind bars.

After a full day in court, Pookie was exhausted. His lawyer was useless to him and he needed to find another one quick. Since this attempt was unsuccessful, Pookie was going to have to go through the process again. He was unsure if he had the energy and patience for it. No matter what, it was important for him to find the strength to push forward. There was no time or room to show weakness.

Settling back into his cell, his cellmate started asking a bunch of questions. That was one thing that annoyed Pookie most was being asked a bunch of questions. He quickly shut him down and turned onto his side in his bed. It didn't matter what position he was in, there was just no getting comfortable. After about half an hour of tossing and turning, Pookie finally fell asleep.

Morning comes and still upset at the fact that his time was not going to be reduced, Pookie loses himself in the remembrance of the night before his court date. His 'favorite' Officer showed up as usual. This time she had plans as she had his cell unlocked for a check. Claiming to have found contraband, she cuffs Pookie and then takes him to the holding area. There was a secret room and about 10 minutes waiting for her to accomplish her goals.

Pookie, knowing what was going down, tried to conceal his excitement. What was there to be excited about in this place? Smiling too hard would surely give away the obvious. They enter the secret room and he pulls out what he found under his pillow. He knew this was the price he had to pay to get the phone, so he gladly obliged. After the deed was done, the Officer pulled the phone out of her pocket and handed it to Pookie.

Walking Pookie back to his cell, she indicated that it was a false alarm and that he was lucky this time. Her body was close to his hands behind his back to help conceal the phone she had given him. She pushes him in his back so as to make him stumble while entering the cell. All of this was part of the semantics to make it not look suspicious and giveaway what they just did.

Now that he has the phone, he can make contacts on his own behalf. First call, a new lawyer, for obvious reasons. Second call, Bonquisha. Getting with her was important so he could work out the master plan for when he gets out. She had to be part of the process because of how well she held things down with Raheim. "Hopefully she will be down." Pookie says out loud to himself.

"Whatcha say?" his cellmate asks of Pookie, all too eagerly.

"Nut'in, man. Ain't nobody talkin' to you!" Pookie shot back. He gave him a look that said 'you know this so why you ask'. "Nosey self! You need to get you some business!" Pookie continued, annoyed.

"Aw man, com'on! I'm jus' try'n' ta be down." his cellmate responded.

"I'm good." Pookie shuts down the conversation. In no way did he want the cellmate in his business nor thinking he was too friendly.

NEW ROLES

On the first work day at the new department, Captain Cooley called KB into his office. He wanted to get to know him a bit more and congratulate him on a job well done for bringing Captain Johnson's wrongful killing to justice. They shared a cigar and had a very long conversation. Captain laid down his expectations, though there wasn't much to be said since KB was the best.

While they were meeting, the team was preparing the conference room for the reception. They even arranged for Alexis to be there, sneaking her past the captain's office in the process. This was easy for them and extra special as they all took an oath to protect and care for Alexis when her father was killed. She was one of them.

KB had no idea this was being planned. He heard a lot of movement going on outside of the captain's office but thought it was business as usual. It was a bit strange to him to have been in the captain's office for so long. Shrugging his shoulders to shake off his suspicions, he continued to enjoy the cigar wishing he had a glass of cognac to go with it.

A knock at the door interrupted their conversation. The receptionist signaled to the captain that it was time. Captain Cooley nodded, then looked at his watch confirming the time. As he began to get up from his chair, he reached out his hand to KB in order to shake it as confirmation of his welcome.

"Let me show you to your office." Captain Cooley says.

As the lead of the department, KB was assigned an office with a window just down the hall from the captain. While walking down the hall, KB is taking note of everything. He quickly assesses the number of desks, papers left on desks that should be locked away, and a number of organizational changes that will need to be made. The captain is pointing out the location of the break room, restrooms, supply rooms, etc., which KB had already taken note of prior to it being mentioned.

"And this is the main conference room where we have our morning meetings." Captain Cooley says while opening the door.

"SURPRISE!!" they all yelled as KB entered the room. The remaining team that was still out on the floor piled in after him. They had stayed behind so it would not appear too obvious that something was going on and giveaway the surprise.

"Oh, no. Oh, my. What??" KB is in shock. He puts his hands on his head in disbelief. Even though he was the best at what he does, he was humble and in no way expected such a huge reception.

Everyone is walking toward him to greet him and shake his hand. They are coming so fast that he does not see Alexis, which was on purpose. She would be the last face he would see. Finally, the last person comes up to shake his hand and as he moves to the side, there she is.

"Babe!!! What are you doing here? How? When? You knew about this? Oh, you got me good!" KB says and starts to tear up as he was overjoyed.

She wraps her arms around his neck and plants a big fat kiss on his lips. The officers and detectives are all saying "Ooooohhhh!" and he begins to blush. For a quick second, they almost forgot that other people were in the room and had to catch themselves.

"Thank you, guys! Thank you! I had no idea. You all really got one over on me, and you can best believe it won't happen again…" KB says as everyone burst into laughter. They enjoy lunch, cake and punch and then presented KB with a plaque and a gift that they all pulled together money to buy.

"Oh, you are too kind." KB tells them while holding back tears. He is not usually an emotional guy, but all of this has been overwhelming, in a good way. With his wife there, this new job and the welcome he received was icing on the cake.

Now that all the celebrating was out of the way, it was time to get acclimated to his new role and team members. He went to his office and set his plaque and gift on the desk, making a mental note to hang the plaque on the wall in the next couple of days. A computer had already been provided for him and was sitting on the desk. Before taking any action on it, he inserted a thumb drive to run a program to check for any bugs.

"Can never be too careful..." he thought to himself while waiting for the program to complete. He also used a special tool to scan the room for any bugs or hidden cameras. Having found no bugs or cameras, KB settles in to begin scheduling one on ones with his team.

"Knock, knock." Alexis appears in KB's doorway to his office. "Off to work so fast!" she pouts.

"Well, I gotta get things rolling." he replies. "Come here." Gesturing for her to meet him at the corner of his desk. She complies. When they are face to face, he turns her around and wraps his arms around her with his hands clasped over her stomach. They savor the moment as they come to the realization that their honeymoon days are over.

"Now what am I going to do all day?" Alexis continued her pouting session.

"You could start your restaurant like you have always talked about." KB replied.

"That is absolutely a great idea! It will surely keep me busy while you are out fighting crime. You just make sure you come home every day!" Alexis says and then plants another kiss on his lips.

"No doubt! Love you Dear!" KB responds.

"Love you too, Dear." Alexis laughs while giving him a big hug before leaving.

He admires her as she is walking away. In the back of his mind, a strange thought appeared. Cocking his head to the side, he notices an extra twist in Alexis' walk. "Hmmmm, I wonder…" he says to himself.

LURKING

Ant was overly excited about his 'date' with Bonquisha last week. He never dreamed he would be on a date with her. Now he was just waiting for another chance to show her that she should choose him to take over her heart. She definitely had his long before Raheim ever proposed to her.

Fresh out the shower and a fresh shave, Ant piles on the smell goods and gets dressed. He was on a mission and half the work was already done for him. She already has a ring so he doesn't have to worry about getting another one, so he thinks. First things first though, he has to win her over.

Hopping in his SUV instead of the car, he heads over to the local flower shop. The shop owner helps him pick out a beautiful bouquet. He agrees with the selection and hopes Bonquisha will as well. Getting back into the SUV, he checks his phone for any missed calls. Wishful thinking had him hoping she may have called for another date. She had to be hungry by now.

Seeing there was no missed calls, he continued with his plan to head over to Bonquisha's home. If she was there, he had it all worked out what he was going to say. It had to be just right so he wouldn't get cussed out, even though showing up unannounced was a sure-fire way to get what he was trying to avoid.

"Um, whatchu' doin' over here?" Bonquisha twists her head and looks Ant up and down like he was crazy. She was just about to leave to start her day of surveillance and didn't need anything to slow her down. This unexpected pop up was doing just that.

Ant being crazy wasn't too far from the truth as he was risking his life in this moment. He didn't care as her hot temper turned him on and sent chills up his spine. With a big cheesy grin, he pulls out the flower bouquet and hands it to her hoping to soften the blow of such an unexpected visit.

"Here. These are for you." He gives her what he thinks is a sexy look while handing her the flowers and continues talking before she can respond. "Now before you say anything, I just wanted to thank you for allowing me to take you out to eat."

"Yeah, whateva!" Bonquisha replies and rolls her eyes at the same time, internally regretting her decision to use him. "Don't be poppin' up ova here!" She yells and turns to lock her door only to realize that she needed to take those flowers inside and put them in water.

"Shoot! This is delaying me!!" She says angrily.

Ant sees his third mistake and is hoping he didn't really mess up. At least she didn't throw the flowers back at him. Maybe he is wearing her down. That was his plan, to keep showering her with kindness until she broke. Then, he would move in for the kill.

"Hey Shorty, I'm sorry, just wanted to express my gratitude. You want to roll with me? I can take you wherever you going. Save you some gas, get you some food…" He tries to recover.

"Nah! I got it. Get gone, na', you holdin' me up!" She pushes him out of the way and runs to her car. Driving off, she looks in the rearview mirror to make sure he is leaving and not following her. After confirming he left, she speeds down the street, flying through the stop sign to make up for lost time.

Ant is going about his day and thinking of his next move. It has to be strategically planned out if he really wanted to win her heart. In the process of thinking, he decides to follow her which is why he slowed down a bit when leaving her home. Following her will give him more insight into what she likes and what she spends her day doing.

A quick U-turn and he's hot on her trail but making sure to keep his distance. He didn't want her to see him. As he is driving, it becomes apparent that Bonquisha is nearing Alexis' home and Ant begins to wonder why. She stops and parks about three houses down forcing him to pull over and park about two houses down from where she parked.

Alexis is seen leaving her home alone. Driving by their vehicles, she is completely oblivious to them. Knowing that Bonquisha would pass by Ant as she turned around to follow Alexis, he quickly backs up to turn down the side street out of view. Waiting for Bonquisha to pass by, he then takes off behind her.

"What in the world is this girl up to?" Ant asks himself. He pops a piece of gum in his mouth and is chewing it like there is no tomorrow. Following behind these two was getting tiring and Ant realizes he has to use the restroom. He turns off the highway and stops at the nearest convenience store.

After using the facilities and buying an energy drink, Ant returns to his vehicle so he could go home. The entire way home, he is thinking about Bonquisha and her obsession with Alexis that he didn't know existed. Helping her with whatever she was trying to do could be his way in to her heart.

New Found Love

It is early in the morning on Sunday. The sun is just rising. Alexis sits up in bed and begins to yawn and stretch. She is careful not to over exert herself as she doesn't want to cause injury to her new found love. Sitting there, staring at KB as he sleeps so peacefully, she ponders how she is going to tell him. She wonders if he is going to be happy or what exactly will be his reaction.

Leaning over, she plants a kiss on his forehead, and whispers "Good morning, Love!" in his ear. He moans and smiles, then turns onto his side. As he drifts back to sleep, Alexis uses this opportunity to start her day and goes into the bathroom to freshen up. She stares at herself in the bathroom mirror. Holding her stomach, she is wondering if anyone can see her small bump which is really only visible to herself as she is only three months.

A shrug of the shoulders satisfies the moment and she heads to the kitchen to make breakfast. Alexis peeks at KB to make sure he is still sleeping. "He has good reason to be so tired." she thinks with a smile, reminiscing about the night before. Sneaking past him quietly while planning what will be for breakfast in her head, she continues downstairs. Arriving in the kitchen, there is a surprise on the kitchen counter.

"When did this get here?" she says out loud, catching herself so she doesn't disturb his sleep. She eyes the small box wrapped in pink paper with a matching bow and a card attached that says 'To my BEAUTIFUL Wife'. After giving it a good look over for a few minutes, she could no longer hold out.

"I guess I should open it." she convinces herself and then proceeds to rip it apart. In the process, she doesn't notice that KB has snuck up behind her. He kisses her on her neck, runs his fingers down her side and grabs her by the waist pulling her closely to him. She pauses for a hot second to take in his aura and then continues tearing off the wrapping.

"Now, you were supposed to wait for me." he tells her.

"Too late!" she replies and continues opening the box with the biggest, cheesiest smile on her face, eyes wide, and laughing with enjoyment.

"So impatient!" he teases her.

Once opened, her mouth drops as her eyes fall on the contents. She grabs the key ring and dangles it in the air. Turning around to face KB, her mouth open and eyes wide as the shock takes over, she immediately plants a big fat kiss on his lips. Screaming and jumping up and down, forgetting about her own surprise for a second, she runs toward the garage.

"OH MY GOD!!!! OH MY GOD!!! I can't believe you got it! OH MY GOD!!" Alexis screams and holds her hand over her mouth. Pressing the button to unlock the doors and get in, she is still in such disbelief. KB had surprised her with the BMW X7 M60i with all the bells and whistles. She slides into the front seat taking it all in and then turns to look in the back.

"Wait…what??...How…." Alexis could hardly speak any words. She gets out and opens the passenger door. There was a car seat in the back that could be used from birth through toddler. She thought it was going to be her surprise, but he knew. She immediately started crying.

KB stood behind her enjoying the moment and holding back his own tears. He was super excited about becoming a father with the love of his life. Shaking his head and holding out his arms to prepare for the embrace once Alexis exited the vehicle. "Rotten! Just Rotten! Nothing but the best for the love of my life and my baby" he says as she jumps into his arms, crying uncontrollably.

"How did you know?" she asked.

"I am a detective. I am trained to know all things." KB replied, thinking back to when he noticed it as she was leaving his office. "Now, let's get to that breakfast you were about to make us. My stomach is growling and we can't keep our little one waiting either." he says while guiding her back into the house and holding her stomach.

Once in the kitchen, she gathers herself and begins to collect all of the ingredients needed to make a spinach, tomato, and cheese omelet with a side of bacon, pancakes, and fresh squeezed orange juice. That's what her taste buds were calling out for her to make, or was it the baby growing inside of her, or just plain greedy.

After breakfast, they get ready for church. During the drive there, KB is unusually quiet, caught up in his own thoughts. Alexis reaches over and turns up the radio to break the silence. She then begins to sing along with the song, one of her favorite gospel songs by her favorite gospel artist. KB grabs her hand and smiles.

They arrive at the church and KB's nerves are getting the best of him. This wasn't like him to be so nervous, but it was important for the next surprise to go off without a hitch. He parks and then goes around the vehicle to open her door and help his precious cargo exit. Doors fling open as they near the doors of the church and they are greeted by the ushers.

"Quick, this way." One of the ushers says to Alexis who turns to look at KB with a hint of confusion. Now she is wondering what else Mr. Smooth has up his sleeve. Her mind is racing trying to figure out what is going on as she follows the usher. Just as she realizes how early they arrived at church, the door to one of the classrooms opens.

"Surprise!" A crowd of church goers yell as she is entering the room. The room is decorated with baby colors as it is still too soon to tell what they are having. A table to the left is filled with gifts and a table to the right is filled with food. She turns around looking for KB who is standing right behind her with his arms wide open.

"Gotcha! I told you I can't be outdone!" KB retorts.

This was payback for the surprise at his office. They enjoy the celebration, opening gifts and eating all the goodies that were brought. Before going in to worship, Alexis pulls KB to the side and stares in his eyes with extreme admiration and love. It was truly a blessed day.

THE RUN IN

Alexis is out shopping again. She stayed shopping when she wasn't volunteering or out with KB. Unbeknownst to her, she had all kinds of company following her every move. For safety reasons, KB had security detail keeping an eye on Alexis. They were hiding in plain sight so as not to draw attention to the possibility that there may be a threat. And of course, there was Bonquisha watching her as well.

"Unh unh, I know she didn't just drive up in that! Always flaunting her newfound happiness and money. Errrybody ain't able!" Bonquisha utters to herself while rolling her eyes. "I think it is time we just so happen to run into each other. She needs to know I am here. This is going to be epic!"

Bonquisha proceeds to walk up to Alexis and then notices two muscular men dressed in polos and slacks inching closer. Seeing this made Bonquisha rethink her game plan. An abrupt about face and quick duck behind the make-up counter gets her out of sight. Carefully, watching the men, she eases out of the store and goes to her car.

Beforehand though, she sneaks a peek at Alexis' new BMW X7. The windows are tinted but she thinks she sees something in the backseat. "Hmmm, too dark, can't make it out…wonder what that is?" Bonquisha says while walking away.

In deep thought, she gets into her car. "Okay, I'm going to have to try that again on a different day. Now that I know what's up, I'll be ready next time." Bonquisha says to herself while sitting in her car waiting for Alexis to finally exit the mall. "What is taking her so long? She has everything already? Who can do that much shopping?" Bonquisha catches herself going on about Alexis and starts to laugh hysterically. As Alexis exits the mall and gets into her new ride, Bonquisha starts her car. "Where to next?" she asks as if someone is in the car listening.

Next stop, the grocery store. One thing Bonquisha missed was her friend's great cooking. Wishing she had paid more attention and learned a few things while watching Alexis in the kitchen made her stomach start to growl. As she parks, the security that was tailing Alexis in the mall pulled into the parking lot. Bonquisha dipped down in her seat so as not to be seen. Once they drive by, she takes note of where they are parked and watches everyone go into the store.

"She has no idea she is being followed. You would think she would be paying more attention. Instead, she walkin' around all oblivious and stuff. I know I taught her betta than that and her father too...." Bonquisha shakes her head and continues to watch.

About ten minutes passed and she decided to go into the store as well. She forgot she needed some items since her cupboard was bare. While walking around the store, Bonquisha is careful not to be seen by the security nor Alexis. After grabbing a few items, she heads to the self-checkout line and hopefully a mad dash to her car. Just as she hits the door of the store, she hears a soft voice try to yell her name.

"Bonquisha?" Alexis yells from the back of the store. "I know I just saw her. Why is she running from me?" Alexis asks herself while trying to catch up to her. Abandoning her basket before going out of the door, she looks left and right outside. "Now where did she go?" Alexis says half out of breath, knowing she should not be running like a crazy person.

Bonquisha quickly ran to the side of the store, out of sight. Bending over, peeking around the corner, she watches Alexis go back into the store. She makes a mad dash to her car, throws the groceries in the back and drives off. In the rearview mirror, she sees the security detail briskly walking outside, canvasing the area. They miss spotting her as she is driving away.

"That was too close for comfort! I'm not ready yet." Bonquisha is taking deep breaths to calm her heart rate and nerves. Driving home, she is thinking about her next move. With all of this intel on Alexis from trailing her every move daily, she is closer to developing her game plan.

Arriving home, she notices a car that slows past her house and then drives off quickly. She takes note of the car, a black sedan with dark tinted windows. Wondering if it was Alexis' security detail or someone else, she shrugs her shoulders and proceeds to go into her home. Locking the door behind her, she takes a look out of the window to make sure no one is there.

MEET UP

Bonquisha is buzzed in through the gates at the prison along with all the other guests for the day. The Officers do their normal check to make sure no weapons or drugs were being smuggled into the prison. After checks were done and all were signed in, they were each led to the waiting area and assigned a seat to wait for the arrival of the prisoner they were visiting.

"Oh, my goodness! This is the worst! Who wants to visit anybody in this place? They need to hire a cleaning crew. Disinfect ten times over, especially before I come up in here again!" Bonquisha says as she is walking to the waiting area. She was really upset because she wished Pookie was dead instead of Raheim, especially since he is the one that brought KB around.

"I don't even know why I am here." She says to herself and ponders leaving. Just as she gets up to do so, the Officer opens the door on the other side of the wall. In walks a group of prisoners, one of whom was Pookie. Bonquisha rolls her eyes as Pookie takes his seat.

Seeing Pookie alive made Bonquisha almost start to cry. 'Keep it ta'getha', keep it ta'getha', she says to herself, batting her eyes to fight back the tears and prevent her mascara from running. She smacks her teeth and then grabs the phone on the wall, rolling her eyes in the process.

"Hey, thanks for coming. How you holding up?" Pookie asks.

"I'm a'ight." Bonquisha responds dryly.

"I know this is not ideal. I'm working on some things. Jus' hol' on." Pookie states. "It's good to see you." he continues.

"Why exactly am I here?" Bonquisha inquires. "An' don't be summoning me like you own me or su'n!" she continues.

"I get it. I know you mad. I miss my cousin too! I was fooled by KB jus' like everybody else. I want to get him jus' like you do!" Pookie responds, trying to reason with Bonquisha.

"Okay, so whatchu' want wit' me?" Bonquisha pushes.

"Look here, Imma' have my people reach out to you. Be looking for a call from my boy." Pookie tells her.

"Ant?!" Bonquisha says a bit too loudly.

"Shhh!!! Not so loud, Shorty!" Pookie replies, his eyes big while looking around to make sure no one heard or paid attention to her.

She really didn't care if anyone heard her. All she knew is that Pookie was on the other side of the glass instead of Raheim and that made her furious. Her blood was boiling inside and she was turning red. She was so hot, that she started to perspire as well.

"Okay, 5 minutes! Wrap it up!" Pookie's 'favorite' officer yelled. She was eyeing them the entire time and smacking her teeth. In her mind, Bonquisha was a threat and she needed to get him away from her.

"Look, he already been bugging the heck out of me. Whatever you got going on, you need to make it clear real soon. I ain't got time for all this! Besides, whatchu' gon' do from in here anyway?" Bonquisha tells Pookie while rolling her eyes.

"Alright, alright! I gotcha'. Don't be in such a rush and all mean. I got you!" Pookie assures her, but she's not buying it.

They hang up the phones to end their conversation. The officer is still eyeing Bonquisha as she is walking away with much attitude. Noticing this, Bonquisha puts a little more twist in her walk to match her attitude. The officer grabs Pookie and pushes him in such a way that he slightly trips and hits his head on the door. She was really thinking there was something between Pookie and Bonquisha and had to let them both know she didn't like it.

Bonquisha turns and sees this. She immediately bursts into laughter to the officer's surprise. Realizing she was wrong for making Pookie hit his head, the officer immediately begins to apologize and check him to determine the seriousness of his injury. Bonquisha is quickly led out of the facility as her outburst of laughter may have been viewed as some sort of diversion.

"Ooohhh, GLAD to be out of there. That is the most horrible place. I don't plan on ever going back there again!!" She says as she gets into her car and drives away. "Now, back to business." Bonquisha whispers.

"Man, what happened to you?" Pookie's cellmate asks.

"Nuthin' man. Leave me alone!!!" Pookie responds and then throws himself on the bed. The rest of the night was spent thinking about how to get back at the officer for what she did to him. She had to pay and all favors for her were canceled, whether it was a benefit to him or not. No one embarrasses him nor inflects harm upon him and gets away with it. She messed up royally.

Pookie was so angry that he kept punching the pillow. He knew this would result in his nosey cellmate asking questions again. As soon as he did, Pookie pulled him off the top bunk down to the floor and then began taking out his anger on him. Officers could be heard running toward the commotion as it was supposed to be lights out for everyone.

The inmate from the cell next to theirs did the secret tap indicating someone was coming. Pookie heard this and snapped out of it. His cellmate climbed back onto the top bunk, curled up and went to sleep, silently crying and vowing to himself to figure out a way to get back at Pookie. Something he knew would be difficult.

Pookie climbed into his bed just in time to avoid being seen by the officers. After they completed checking to ensure all inmates were in their beds and behaving, they returned to their posts. Feeling a bit more satisfied and calmed, Pookie turned onto his side and went to sleep.

SUSPICIONS

KB arrived at the meeting place to discuss the events of the week with the men assigned to keep an eye out for Alexis. He became more furious as he listened to their accounts of what happened. While they were talking, he was already devising an even greater plan to keep her safe.

"I knew it! Alexis kept telling me she had this strange feeling. That is probably who left that gift in front of our door when we returned from our honeymoon. We still haven't opened it. I hid it from Alexis so she could forget about it." KB rambles on and on in out loud thought processing mode.

He proceeds to walk to his car and open the trunk to grab the aforementioned gift. Handing it to the men, he had them take it to be checked for fingerprints. He had already checked it to make sure it wasn't a bomb. Now it could be opened to determine the contents as well.

Given the duties of his job, KB could not afford to take any chances. Everyone knew who he was after taking down Raheim so there was sure a target on his back. Alexis is his everything and he had to make sure she was not harmed as part of any retaliation for what he does every day.

After meeting with the team and giving them additional instruction, he makes a mental note to beef up the security at home. Next step is to also check Alexis' phone for any type of tracking programs. That had to be the only way Bonquisha was able to show up so often in the same place, KB thought to himself.

KB arrives at work and runs right into the conference room for the morning meeting. His assistant greeted him with a cup of coffee, to which he added a harmless solution to check for any poisons prior to drinking it. No matter what, he was always suspicious of everyone, except Alexis.

The meeting is now over and he can start the next phase of his day. No one knew about his meeting before the morning meeting. This was something he was paying for out of his own pocket and did not involve the team from his office. There could be leaks in the department and he had to be sure there were no leaks on his security detail that was keeping tabs on his precious wife.

One by one, KB calls members of the team into his office for the weekly meeting with each. Getting to know them was very important to the process of building the trust that was going to be needed as they worked together. He took notes as they talked both on paper and mentally as he noticed all their mannerisms. It was as if he was a human lie detector machine. He had a way of making them feel comfortable enough to make slight mistakes that revealed their character.

Lunch time came quickly and KB sought to use this time to check on Alexis. He met her for lunch around the corner at a nearby restaurant where he could enter from the back door. There was a special table in the back set aside for him to use whenever needed. It was secluded so that no one could see him.

"Hello Dear." KB says as he leans over to give her a kiss.

"Hi Honey Bear." Alexis returns after the kiss. "How's your day been?" she asks.

"Much better now that I am with you." KB responds. "I took the liberty of preordering." He continues.

"Thank you, Honey! You are so sweet and thoughtful and always know what I want. I love how you take care of me." Alexis replies.

"Of course! Nothing but the best for the best!" KB lets the words roll out with ease while holding her hands and staring into her eyes. He is thinking about how much he can't live without her and especially not now since she is carrying his first child.

"Oh, let me see your phone right quick." He says while holding out his hand to wait for her to hand it to him. Once he has it, he scrolls through it looking for tracking apps. Coming across the phone tracker app, he inquires if she is still using it and who else may have access to it.

"You know what? Bonquisha and I set that up a long time ago. I haven't used it in a while." She responds.

KB continues to examine the app and sees that there has been some recent activity. It shows that Bonquisha has been logged in and checking up on Alexis. Thinking to himself, this is just what he thought was going on and how she was able to keep up with Alexis. He shows what he found to Alexis.

"OH MY GOSH!!!! Are you serious? She's been tracking me all this time?" Alexis responds with a combination of fear, anger, and confusion in her tone.

"You never used this app yourself, did you?" KB asks.

"No, not really. I would only check it every now and then to make sure she was good. But that's it. So, if she has been following me around, could that explain the strange feeling I have been having?" Alexis asks, her mind racing and heartbeat picking up the pace to match.

All of a sudden, she grabs her chest and starts to breath more intensely. She's trying to calm herself down as KB gets up to wrap his arms around her and help her slow her breathing. They didn't want anything to cause harm to the baby so it was important for her to get things under control.

They slowly exit the restaurant through the back. KB has his security detail team on the line so they can meet them and immediately take her to the hospital as a precaution. He heads to the hospital taking an alternate route, keeping the lead detail member on the phone the entire way. Alexis' phone was in his hand as well and he noticed the tracker was in action.

KB let the lead know that he was going to take a slight detour and will be at the hospital shortly. He makes a quick right turn and proceeds to the nearest inconspicuous spot to park. Within five minutes, Bonquisha appears as expected. She is slowly approaching KB's vehicle and then quickly darts to the left. While she is speeding off into the other direction, KB turns off the tracker on Alexis' phone for now.

BLAST FROM THE PAST

Bonquisha makes it home after an almost awful ordeal that could have been the end of her plan. Seeing KB parked where she thought Alexis might have been really spooked her. This means he must be on to her and trying to figure out what she was up to by tracking Alexis around.

"His security detail must have spilled the beans about my close encounters. I have got ta' be mo' careful than that. Going to hav' ta' change up my plans and speed up this process. But everything has to be just right for when I make my move..." Bonquisha rattles on to herself. Again, no one is there to listen.

She realizes that she is talking to herself again and then begins to feel hunger pains. First thought was to call Ant and demand he take her to eat. Then quickly changing her mind just as fast as the thought entered. She didn't want Ant to think that there were any feelings developing. Plus, Raheim had stashed money in her apartment that wasn't found by the cops after everything went down.

"Hmmm.... what do I want to eat today? I think I will have some salmon and broccoli in some of that fancy butter sauce.... Yeah, that sounds good." Bonquisha says to herself as she goes into her closet to change clothes.

After getting ready, she heads out the door. Stopping dead in her tracks, she sees the black sedan parked across the street. Reaching in her purse in preparation for what might be about to go down, she sees the car door open. The tension that had built up in her neck immediately relaxed when she saw it was Stephen.

Removing her hand from her purse and bursting into laughter as he approaches her. She is wondering what the H-E-double hockey sticks he is doing there. Why had he been semi-stalking her these last few weeks. All these questions began to flood her brain.

"Heyyyyyy girl! What is going on with you? How have you been?" Stephen says as he opens his arms to give Bonquisha a hug.

Bonquisha returns the hug but still a bit suspiciously. It has been some years since she last saw Stephen and often wondered how he was doing. He was

Alexis' love for a while until that fateful day. Alexis went to Stephen's apartment to surprise him and cook dinner for him. She had a key and let herself in just as she normally would. Only this time, maybe she should have called before she went there.

Upon walking into the room, Alexis sees Stephen on the couch and some other woman straddled across his lap. They were both naked and almost unbothered by the sudden unexpected intrusion. Alexis dropped the bags she had in her hands. Her mouth also dropped and her eyes widened. She turned and ran down the stairs, got back in her car, and drove home crying the entire way.

After that incident, Alexis swore off men forever, until KB came along. Thinking about this made Bonquisha very upset, both at Stephen and at KB. She punched Stephen in the chest several times in retaliation for the pain he caused her once upon a time best friend. Then she reached in her purse again, but stopped before anything further could happen that would ruin her chances to get revenge for KB's wrongful killing of Raheim.

"What are you doing here and what do you want?" Bonquisha questions Stephen.

"I moved back to town recently. I heard about what happened. How you holdin' up?" Stephen asks.

"I'm fine. Whatchu want?" Bonquisha pushes the issue.

"Okay, okay, chill! I'm just catching up with old friends." Stephen replies.

"Old friends? We ain't old friends!" Bonquisha retorts.

"Look, I'm just trying to see what's up with Alexis." Stephen begins.

"Oh okay, now we gettin' to the real deal!" Bonquisha cut him off, rolled her eyes and crossed her arms.

"How is she doing?" Stephen inquires with sincerity in his voice.

"I'onno! You can creep up on her jus' like you been creeping around and popping up on me!" Bonquisha replies. "Now you holdin' me up! I'm hungry and about to be hangry!" she snaps.

"Alright, Alright! I get it. I know I hurt her and you will do whatever to protect her. I don't know what came over me…. well, I guess I do…it was the whole celibacy thing…. a man has needs…" he rambles on and on hoping to convince Bonquisha to help him.

She pushes him out of the way as she is getting in her car. Slams the door shut, but rolls down her window. Turning to look at him while starting her car, she starts to think about how she might actually can use him, especially seeing how desperate he was. This might could work out in her favor.

"I can't make no promises, but I might can help you out. I'll call you, DON'T call me nor come by here again!!" she says before driving away.

"YES!" he says and pumps his fist in excitement. That was all he needed was a window of a chance to get in Alexis' good graces. Hope is all he had to hold onto to try to win her back. Little did he know that it would be almost impossible. Not only because she and KB were married, but also because she had an anger inside of her that had been pushed deep down and was waiting to come out at the right opportunity.

Stephen gets in his car and drives off a happy man, singing all the way to his new apartment. Arriving home, he noticed a couple of black suburban vehicles had been following him but kept it moving as he pulled into the parking lot. He shrugged it off and went inside his apartment to begin planning his approach for the day when he would be able to reconnect and rekindle what he had with Alexis.

ANT MAKES HIS MOVE

"It's time. I have taken her out too many times. I must be wearing her down. So, I'm going to ask to be her man. Then we can run this thing together. I know she about that money, so, it should be a no brainer." Ant says to himself while getting ready to leave to meet Bonquisha for an early evening dinner.

Bonquisha had just called him and demanded he meet her at a restaurant across town. This was perfect timing as he was actually about to reach out to her. They both have different motivations for getting with each other. Time will tell how it will all play out. In the meantime, they are both using each other.

The drive across town seemed to take forever. Traffic was a hot mess. Being stuck in it gave Ant time to think about his game plan and how he is going to ask the question. Wondering in his mind what she will say, he veers into the other lane slightly. Horns blowing brought him out of his trance.

"Oh Lord! My bad!" Ant says to the drivers in the cars around him as if they could hear him. They might not be able to hear but they could see his gesture requesting his forgiveness. He wanted to avoid a case of road rage, especially since one guy seemed to be yelling obscenities toward him. Back in his own lane now, he is focused on making it to his destination, not only alive, but on time as well. Bonquisha had a short fuse and he didn't want to be late.

He arrives at the restaurant with ten minutes to spare. Checks the mirror, applies some Carmex, and hops out of the vehicle. Making sure to lock it, he then proceeds to enter the restaurant and is looking around the entire time taking in his surroundings. Something Raheim taught him. They were friends and he learned a lot from Raheim and until now he felt bad about wanting his girl. Ant believes that Raheim would want him to take care of her and it was his duty. It was the only way he could pay Raheim back for all he did for him when he was alive. Raheim respected Ant and made sure everyone else did too. He didn't allow anyone to treat Ant different because of his height.

As soon as he steps inside the restaurant, the greeter welcomes him and immediately escorts him to a table in the back. How special he felt at this moment. He was smiling from ear to ear and had to compose himself just before arriving at the table. Bonquisha was already seated and looking quite beautiful to him. She was dressed up a little bit this time. It wasn't for him though; the restaurant was that type of venue. It was just romantic enough to set the mood for him to ask her the important question.

He attempts to greet her with a hug, but she thwarts that effort and holds out her hand to shake his. As usual, he is sitting with his back to everyone else in the restaurant which was a bit uncomfortable, but he knew she wouldn't let anything go down. Relaxing into his seat, ready to eat, Ant begins to review the menu. It wasn't necessary because Bonquisha had already ordered and drinks were already being placed on the table for them.

She specifically told him to be there ten minutes after she would get there to help speed up the process. Being as hangry as she was, especially after being delayed by the surprise appearance by Stephen, she couldn't wait for Ant to arrive to order. He was typical and she knew what he would get so she took the liberty to give the waiter the order for the both of them.

"I'm so glad you called. I was jus' 'bout ta' call you." Ant says in between sips of his beverage. "Ooohh, this is good!" he says while smacking to get the full effect of the flavor.

She was trying to get him to level up and be more sophisticated. Even though she didn't like him, he was being nice. He was someone to talk to instead of the walls in her appointment. His height was a deal breaker for her so no consideration of this becoming anything more than two people filling up on good grub! Little did she know that Ant had other plans in mind.

"So, as I was saying, I am so glad you called. We have been kicking it for a bit. I have been enjoying getting to know you." Ant begins.

"Oh unh unh! Wait a minute! I 'no you NOT catching feelings?" Bonquisha interrupts.

"Hol' on Shorty!" He interrupts back.

"Really?" she says in response to him calling her Shorty given his height deficiency.

"I do like you. Always did and I think you know that." Ant says with a bossed-up tone. "Now, I think it's time we put a name on this. I want you to be my girl." Ant says. In his mind he is thinking this is not how he wanted it to go, how he wanted to ask her. But Bonquisha is not one to be soft with, she likes to be handled, he has learned in this moment. He can see why Raheim was able to hook her and he is going to have to be more like Raheim if he wants to keep her.

"You know what? I'll think about it." she says to his surprise.

Ant did a double take with a look on his face that said 'whatchu say?'. He couldn't believe she didn't outright say no. An answer of 'I'll think about it' was music to his ears and the door he needed. More pressure was about to be poured on each time they hooked up. Bonquisha had no idea what she just signed up for with that response.

TASK FORCE

The task force assembled at KB's new office was ready to put plans together to take down their next big target. Each member was selected by KB based on the special skills they possessed and past experience. The process seemed to take forever, but he had to be sure he could trust them in the heat of the moment and trust them to be discreet. One wrong move at the most inopportune time could jeopardize everything they were working on and cause numerous casualties.

To date, KB had not lost one member of any of the teams he worked with or led. It was very important for him to keep this record going. Every team member had to return home to their families without injury. KB would have it no other way, especially because he needed to do the same. This was even more of necessity with his new baby on the way.

Those who were not selected sat around the office with the long face. Everyone wanted to work with KB. He assured them that everyone would get the opportunity to participate at some point in time depending on the circumstances. This was stated to avoid having anyone turn and take to the other side out of jealousy.

Captain Cooley had to sign off on every selection. He trusted KB's judgement and therefore the approval process was swift. Captain met with each team member individually to provide their approval and give them the speech that basically said no mess ups or else. He wanted to make sure everyone knew the consequences if they disobeyed any order given by KB.

Now that all of the formalities were complete, KB called everyone on the team into the conference room for a quick meeting. It had been a long day and he wanted to set the tone for the rest of the week before everyone went home. To their surprise upon entering the room, they are met with the aroma of a catered meal from his favorite Italian restaurant. Lasagna, spaghetti, chicken alfredo, breadsticks, salad, tea, and lemonade were on the menu. Desserts included lemon cake, cheesecake, and chocolate cake.

"Enjoy! First thing in the morning at o-five hundred hours, be at the gym ready for a workout." KB says with a smile.

"So, you want us to eat alllllll this good food and then be ready to work out at five o'clock in the morning?" one of the team members asked.

"Yep!" KB replied, still smiling. No one got the joke but him.

"Okay, you da' BOSS!" the outspoken team member responded.

They all fixed a hefty plate to sit, eat, and fellowship. Many taking personal calls on their phones to let their loved ones know they were on the way as soon as they finished stuffing their faces. Even after they ate, there was still enough food left for each member to take home a plate, and they did just that.

KB felt it was important to take care of his team. This ensured they took care of him, and each other. This meal was the start of the necessary bonding and creation of loyalty that would be the ultimate decision maker in the heat of the moment. Every move KB made had a purpose.

He wrapped up the day and gathered his things to head home. As he approached his car, a huge smile came over his face. In about forty-five minutes, KB would arrive home to his beautiful wife and baby. Aside from getting his man when working a case, nothing excited him more.

He took a different route home every day just in case someone decided to lose their mind and follow him. No one would be able to track his every move. Passing by the flower shop on the route he took this day, he decided to stop and get a bouquet of flowers. The owner created a nice assortment of pink and purple flowers with dark pink roses weaved throughout. She handed the bouquet to KB with a smile as he handed her the money along with a considerable sized tip.

He got back in the car and as he began to drive off, the phone rings. It is his granny's nursing home. A sudden feeling of worry came over him. He hated to leave her and planned on moving her closer once he got settled, especially so she could see the baby once born. Quickly saying a brief prayer before answering the phone, he took a deep breath and then answered the call.

"Hello." KB says.

"Yes, Mr. Bowman?" the female voice on the other end says with hesitation.

"This is he. How can I help you?" he replies.

"Yes, your grandmother was saying she wanted to talk to someone named Todd?" she replies, questioning the ask.

He releases a sigh of relief as the worst possible reason for the nursing home to be calling crossed his mind. His heart rate was going a mile a minute and pounding so loudly that he thought the nurse could hear it. The sound was only in his ears and he took a couple of deep breaths to calm it down.

"Oh, okay, yes, that is my brother. He was killed a long time ago. She confuses us all the time. Can you put her on the phone?" KB asks.

"Yes, sir. Hold the line please." she responds. "Ma'am, here you go." KB could hear the nurse state to his granny before handing her the phone.

"Granny! How are you? I miss you!" KB says.

"Todd, is that you?" she asks.

"Granny, this is KB, your favorite!" he responds.

"Oh, okay baby. How you doing?" she replies.

"I'm good. You not giving them a hard time, are you?" KB asks.

"No baby, you know I'm not. They giving me a hard time. Won't let me rest. Won't let me talk to Todd. Keep giving me Jello." she rambles on and on while KB listens the rest of his way home.

"Okay, granny. You keep being good over there. I hope to come see you soon." KB says as he pulls into his driveway.

"Okay baby." she says as they both hang up the phone.

"Home, sweet home!" KB says while getting out of the car to go into the house. "What a day!" he says as he is greeted with a juicy kiss from Alexis.

IT'S TIME

"OH NOOO!" Alexis screams as she is walking toward the kitchen. She is holding her belly and walking gingerly. The other hand is gliding along the wall to help give her more support.

KB is sitting on the couch reading the newspaper, something he rarely gets to do. This was the first time he decided to enjoy some quiet time while Alexis slept in for a change. He hears her scream and jumps up from the couch like someone was breaking into the house.

"WHAT?!!" he yells back.

"I…I think it's TIMMMMEEE…." Alexis belts out, sounding like she is in pure agony.

"OHHHH OOKKKAAYYY. UH, What I do? What I do?" he nervously responds.

She stops in her tracks and looks at him with a look that said 'Really?!'. She begins moving again and all of a sudden, a strange and really warm liquid starts to run down her legs. She looks down in disgust and starts to cry.

"Ewwww....what tha'...Oh LURD" she says.

KB almost passes out at the sight of it. He is normally Mr. Cool, but this is the first time in his life he was lost for what to do. They had a game plan and talked it over frequently, but in the moment, all that planning went by the wayside. He slaps his face to get himself together.

"Okay, okay. I got this." KB tells himself. By the time he pulls himself together, Alexis is already at the door and an ambulance is already pulling into the driveway. She knew he wouldn't be able to handle it, so as soon as she felt that first pain, she called 9-1-1. It was perfect timing when they arrived.

"Babe, when did you call for the ambulance? That's what I was supposed to do." KB asks.

She was shocked. This was the second time he didn't call her 'Dear'. It was kind of funny, but strange. She liked it and it made her smile in the midst of all the pain she was experiencing. That made it hard for her to be annoyed by him in that moment.

KB opened the door to allow the paramedic to enter. He made sure he knew all of the EMS team before allowing them to proceed. After, looking around outside for any dangers and making sure his security detail was also on point, he ran back inside to grab Alexis' bag. It had been pre-packed and was waiting by the door in case she was home alone when this happened.

The paramedic grabbed Alexis and gently helped her to get on the gurney. Secured, she is then rolled and loaded into the back of the ambulance. One of KB's security detail members is tasked to ride with her. KB gets into the BMW X7 he bought Alexis and follows the ambulance to the hospital.

With all of the commotion, no one noticed Bonquisha was parked down the street. Taking it all in, she was both excited and jealous. She had been watching everything unfold and knew it would be time soon for Alexis to have that bundle of joy. She couldn't help but wonder if they might could have been pregnant at the same time. Thinking of Raheim's proposal and the fact that he was no longer alive made her tear up. She followed the entourage to the hospital while fighting back the tears and memories.

They all arrive at the hospital. KB pulls up behind the ambulance and one of his security detail members opens his door so he could go and park the vehicle for him. KB grabs Alexis' bag and heads into the hospital. The remaining security detail begins posting up in various places throughout the hospital. One of them notices Bonquisha parked in the parking lot and alerted everyone.

KB was too distracted to be concerned with Bonquisha. Plus, he knew that his team had an eye on her. He proceeded to go into the room where Alexis had been wheeled to and transferred from the gurney to a bed in preparation for delivery. It wouldn't be long now and KB was the most nervous he had ever been in his life.

Hours later, and after much screaming, sweating, tears and squeezing KB's hand off, the baby was finally born. Out of breath and tired from the ordeal, Alexis falls asleep. KB is holding their new bundle of joy and following behind the doctors and team as they roll Alexis to her room for recovery. The baby stayed with them in the room as KB was not allowing her to leave their site.

Yep, it's a girl!

Alexis awakes after what seemed like days. That was the best sleep she had in a long time. Too bad it was going to be a while before she has that type of sleep again. She sits up carefully and assesses the room. It was full of balloons and flowers congratulating her and KB on their new baby girl. KB is sitting in the chair next to her bed holding the baby and half falling asleep.

"DEAR!" she says, half serious and half laughing. She wished she could grab her phone to snap a picture but it was too far for her to reach. One of the security detail members, a female, was also in the room. Alexis became aware of their existence during the ambulance ride. She signaled for her to grab the phone for her and was able to snap a picture just in time before KB woke up.

"Hey Babe!" KB says with a smile. He gets up and kisses her on the forehead and then hands the baby over to her.

"So, what shall we call her?" Alexis asks. They had not yet decided on a name. So much was going on that there wasn't really time to figure that out. Now that she is here, things seemed to slow down for a bit so they could think.

"How about Beautiful?" KB asks.

Alexis turns up her nose and shakes her head to indicate that was not the name she had in mind. They ponder and toss names back and forth for another hour. Finally, they agree on a name.

"Beautiful!" They both say at the same time.

A couple days pass and it is time to go home. While they are preparing to leave, they hear the nurses running around. KB draws his weapon and runs to the door to peer out of the window. He leaves the security detail team member in the room to go investigate the issue. Relief came over him as he learned that another patient woke up and didn't see her baby near her and was having a fit. He returns to the room to gather Alexis, Beautiful, and all their things so they could go home.

FREE AT LAST

Pookie has been in good spirits as of late. He got a new lawyer after making a few phone calls. This lawyer had a team that left no stone unturned. They went to work right away to find a loophole to help get him out of prison. He had been in there long enough and was ready to get out.

In his opinion, they didn't have enough on him for him to serve ten years. The judge was punishing him for what Raheim did since she couldn't punish Raheim. Pookie felt he just happened to be in the wrong place at the wrong time. Shooting back at the cops that day was self-defense since he was being shot at first.

His next day in court was fast approaching, but couldn't be fast enough. Pookie was ready to get away from his used to be 'favorite' officer. She kept making advances at him, making him real uncomfortable. He regretted he ever used her and gave her the pleasure she desired, even if he did benefit from it.

The day finally arrived and it didn't take long. Not only was his lawyer and team early, they were already approaching the judge with a motion to have Pookie's sentence downgraded to probation. He had no priors, it wasn't proved that he had killed anyone on the day of the raid, and was only there to visit his cousin. Being seen riding around town with his cousin was not a crime either. Since when did being family become a crime?

As Pookie was brought to the table to join his lawyer and team, he barely had time to sit down. The judge was already reviewing the information and in process of making her decision. She asked Pookie to remain standing.

"In light of the motion brought before the court today, and after further review of the previous evidence submitted, the court has decided to grant the request to reduce the sentence of Raymond Clarence Smith, III, to probation with two hundred fifty hours of community service," the judge says and then bangs the gavel.

"Next case!" she continued, as the bailiff proceeded to walk toward Pookie and his team so they could be escorted out of the courtroom.

Pookie falls over and pumps his fists in exhilaration. This is just the break he needed and it couldn't have come soon enough. He needed to get back out there to establish himself as the man, but had to be discreet since he knew he was going to be watched closely. 'But like Grandma always said, where there's a will, there's a way', he thought to himself.

Finally about to be free, he gathers all his belongings and throws up the peace sign to the officers. Relief comes over him as he walks toward the door to be released. He doesn't look back because he had no plans to return to that awful place. Not having to see his 'favorite' officer was the best part of leaving. She was standing in the doorway looking like she just lost her lunch watching him walk away.

Outside the gates, Ant was waiting for him. Pookie hopped in the ride and they gave each other dap. As Ant drove off, Pookie rolled down the window and raised his arm outside of it. He threw a few wayward hand gestures toward the onlooking officers and inmates who were out on the yard. Pulling his arm back inside, he rolled up the window and they sped off, burning rubber with the tires.

"Where to man?" Ant asks.

"Mannnn, you already 'no! First stop is mom's house. I need to eat!!!" Pookie responds. "An' put ya' foot in it!" Pookie urges. Ant was the only person alive who knew where Pookie's mom lived. This was on purpose for both of their protection.

Two hours later, they arrive at Pookie's mom's home. Ant was glad because Pookie had fell asleep and was snoring like there was no tomorrow. He also needed to take a bath because he smelled like prison and now had Ant's vehicle smelling like prison too. Ant tried to spray air freshener and had placed a fresh pine scented tree to hang from the mirror. It didn't help.

"Man, wake up! We here!" Ant says with just a bit too much attitude.

Pookie turned and looked at Ant with the meanest expression Ant had ever seen him make. This moment was the moment that Pookie needed to begin his dominance and reign on the outside world. Ant's tone set something off inside of Pookie and he soon regretted talking to Pookie that way.

"You can leave!" Pookie says without looking back at Ant as he grabs his things and gets out of the vehicle. There was already a nice ride stored at his mom's house, hidden out of sight. No one knew about it so it will be easy for him to roll up in it and catch a few folks off guard.

Ant drives away just as Pookie is entering his mom's house. She always had food ready in the event someone might come by so he knew he was about to throw down. His mom sees him and immediately begins to cry. She raises her hands to put her arms around Pookie as she couldn't believe he was really there.

"Come on. Sit down. Eat. You looking too thin." she says.

He knew not to talk back and to just do as she says. She was the real OG and he knew it. The food was smelling so good, you could smell it down the road. It was like it called you to her driveway. Just like he remembered and dreamed of while in prison, she sets down a plate of roast beef and gravy over rice, sweet potatoes, greens, baked beans, and two freshly made homemade yeast rolls with a special honey cinnamon butter drowning over the top of them. Following that was a big glass of sweetened iced tea with a touch of lemon.

"MOM!!!!" Pookie yells with excitement like a little kid. "You did that!!! I don't think I can eat anymore." he continued.

Before he could say anything else she plops down in front of him a big bowl of apple cobbler and ice cream. While most people raved over peach cobbler, Pookie's favorite was apple cobbler. No one could make it like his mom, no matter how hard they tried.

Too Late to Turn Back

Bonquisha left the hospital after causing a stir just to get a look at Alexis and her new baby. She was able to slip past KB's special team members by causing a diversion on another floor. The black hat she wore was pulled down so that her eyes could not be seen. A new wig was also part of the disguise along with a fake pregnant belly. Needless to say, she had it all worked out.

Seeing Alexis so happy made her sad and seeing her new bundle of joy made her lonely. She longed for Raheim to be by her side and was missing him dearly. The drive home was difficult as she fought back the tears. This was not her usual self which she lost when Raheim was killed. She needed to get herself together.

After what seemed like a trip around the world, Bonquisha arrives home. She throws herself on the couch as if to have her own temper tantrum. The remote control was on the floor by the couch. She grabs it and points it at the television to turn it on and imagines she is taking out KB in the process.

Taking him out was the only way she would feel better and maybe get her friend back.

Stopping on the news, a story catches her eye. She had no idea what was being reported had occurred and it was just what she needed. Now she is sitting up at attention and her brain is running in circles processing what she is seeing and hearing on the news. For sure she would have been called about this, but nothing yet.

"What???!! Pookie got out? Hunh!" Bonquisha says to herself. "Ant, I must call Ant." She continues.

Before calling Ant, she goes to the bathroom. All the water and energy drinks she had during her surveillance was working its way down and out. Walking into the bathroom she is startled by the image looking back at her in the mirror as she forgot she was still in disguise. She burst into laughter and for the first time she laughed harder than she ever had before.

Bent over in pain, she composed herself and wiped the tears that were streaming down from her eyes. She couldn't tell if it was from laughing or crying.

The makeup she had on started to smear as she was wiping her face. She hopped in the shower to wash away all of the pain she was feeling. No matter how hard she scrubbed, it seemed to just linger.

All fresh and clean and ready to go, Bonquisha calls Ant so he can take her to dinner. She had no idea what Ant was up to other than to get with her like he always dreamed of doing. It seemed like the phone didn't get a chance to ring before he answered. Oh yeah, he was sitting by the phone waiting on her call.

"Ey, I'm ready to eat! I'll let you surprise me. See if you been paying attention to what I like." she says before he can get any words out.

"Alright, bet! Come on over then." he responds, trying not to sound too overly excited.

"Come over? Whatchu think this is?" she asks, of course with her head twisted to the side.

"Yeah! Come OVER." Click. He hung up before she could give any further push back, excited at the fact that he was able to pay her back for hanging up on him.

She reluctantly heads over to Ant's house. The radio is blasting in the car so that she can relax her mind on the way there. She even belted out a few bars of her favorite rap song. So as not to seem too hungry, she had a snack on the way. A quick spray of her breath with the mint shot and a peppermint for extra effect hid the smell of the snack she just had.

Arriving and pulling into the driveway, she checks the mirror to make sure everything is in tack. In the back of her mind the question of why she even cared kept circling. Shrugging it off, she grabs her purse, making sure she had all necessary protection inside of it and gets out.

Ant opens the door three seconds before she knocks. As she is stepping inside, she is taking in her surroundings and making mental notes in case things get out of hand. He leads her to a table that has been set with wine glasses, candles, and roses. Pulling out a chair and gesturing for her to sit down, he flashes her a big smile.

"Welcome to my humble abode! Have a seat, get comfortable." he says all in one breath.

"Okay." she responds with hesitation. "It smells good. I didn't know you could cook." she compliments him. All that did was stroke his ego and make him think he had a chance.

"Of course. I gotta eat, so I gotta cook. Self-taught, too." he replies.

He brings over a bottle of her favorite wine and pours some in the wine glasses then places the bottle in the ice bucket. Then he runs back into the kitchen and begins to plate the food, stopping briefly to bring over to the table the croissants and butter. He had planned a four-course meal that was sure to impress.

"So, what's on the menu?" Bonquisha asks while eyeing the croissants. They looked light, crispy and buttery, just like she liked them. 'Hmmm, so he was paying attention,' she thought to herself.

"Nothing but the best for you!" he responds.

They sit and enjoy crawfish beignets for the appetizer followed by a Caesar salad. For the main dish, he prepared grilled salmon with asparagus and mashed potatoes with brown gravy. The dessert was the best part of the meal. Before serving it, he poured them each another glass of wine.

"And the piece of resistance…" Ant says before presenting the dessert. This is his most famous item of them all. "Homemade cheesecake with strawberries and strawberry glaze and a little chocolate and caramel syrups drizzled on both sides of the plate for dipping." he says as he places the plate in front of her.

That was it! That was all she needed. Anything she may have been worried about or sad about all left her mind. She slowly enjoyed every bit of that cheesecake. The plate was so clean, Ant didn't need to wash it.

"Everything was delicious! You really know how to treat a girl. Thanks for paying attention to the detail. This is exactly what I needed." Bonquisha states.

Before they knew it, they were all over each other and passionately kissing. To her surprise, she came to realize Ant was very strong as he picked her up and carried her to his bedroom. She never expected this nor wanted this, but in the heat of the moment, it was too late to turn back.

New Beginnings

Now that it appeared as if Ant and Bonquisha were in a relationship, Bonquisha started to think of how she could use this to her advantage. Ant was Pookie's right hand and now that Pookie was out, she could make her move. First, she needed to see what Pookie was thinking.

"Ant! Why you ain't tell me Pookie was out? When you was gon' tell me dat? You di'n't think it was important?" Bonquisha rattles off questions quickly not giving Ant time to respond.

"Hey Shorty, I didn't know you didn't know." he responds.

"So, where he holdin' up at?" she asks.

"His momma house for now." he replies.

"We need to set up a meeting. Handle dat." she demands.

"Aight." Ant replies while looking at her sideways. He wasn't going to keep being disrespected and having people talk to him any kind of way. It was time out for that. He just needed a little bit more time to get that rock off her finger.

They both leave the restaurant in their separate vehicles and go their separate ways.

Bonquisha was still somewhat in denial about the feelings she was starting to develop for Ant. She tried very hard to be tough and be rude so as to prevent from catching feelings. 'Of all people, why Ant?' she thought to herself.

Ant was smiling the whole way home. He had a particular mission in mind but given that he always liked her, it was really hard to keep that mission at the forefront of what he was trying to do. His thoughts were interrupted by his phone ringing. He looked down to see who it was and swerved a bit.

"Hey man, what's up?" Pookie says as Ant answers the phone.

"Can't call it. What up tho?" Ant responds.

"Roll through and pick me up from moms." Pookie demands.

"Mannnn, I was just about to call you. I'll be there in thirty minutes." Ant says and hangs up.

He arrives at Pookie's mom's house and Pookie is already walking out. He had a ride, but wasn't ready to use it yet. Ant is hoping Pookie is in a good mood while he realizes he is turning into what Pookie used to be for Raheim. Part of him was upset about it and part of him thought of how it made him next in line should anything happen.

"Where we headed?" Ant asks Pookie.

"Just ridin' fa now." Pookie responds.

"Okay, cool. Yeah, so, I got with Bonquisha." Ant says, the statement had a double meaning to him.

"Oh yeah?" Pookie responds.

"Yeah, man. She wanna get with you, set up a meeting." Ant continues.

"Okay, that's what's up. We headed to her house then." Pookie confirms.

They drive to Bonquisha's house after Ant sends her a text to let her know they are on the way. Pookie gets on the phone to start setting up other meetings, pulling his crew together. Ant is listening and taking note.

Finally, they arrive at Bonquisha's. Ant is tired from all the driving. As they approach, the door opens to let them inside. Seeing Pookie was triggering for her but it was necessary to meet up and solidify a game plan to get back the guy who took out the love of her life.

She blocks Ant from showing any affection upon entering as she didn't want Pookie to know what was up. Word in the street was getting around though as they were seen out and about a couple of times. They tried to be discreet, but people are nosey and loved to gossip.

Pookie helped himself to a beverage that Bonquisha had set out. She kept the good stuff hidden in the back of the cabinet as she had no plans to share it. This was not a special occasion nor one of her pity parties. A few bowls of snacks were sitting on the table to which Pookie also helped himself. He was feeling real comfortable, thinking it was okay since he was Raheim's cousin.

"Okay, let's make this quick. I ain't got all day to be kickin' it with you two!" Bonquisha barks.

They talk for a couple of hours working out a game plan to get back at KB. The plan had to be flawless. All of the months of surveillance proved to be helpful and made it easy to figure out each move in the process. While that was the focus of both Bonquisha and Pookie, Ant was thinking of other things. His attention stayed on the ring on Bonquisha's hand so he was half listening.

Pookie hit Ant on the arm. "Pay attention!" he said.

"Man, I got it!" Ant says, although he was not telling the truth.

They finish the meeting and planning. Ant and Pookie get up so they can leave. Next stop was to help Pookie get a place in town. Ant had scoped out a couple of places just before Pookie got out so they went by to look at them.

As they arrived at the first place, Pookie immediately began to shake his head no to indicate he didn't like it. So, they kept driving. The second location was not too far from the first. This one grabbed Pookie's attention, so they pulled into the driveway. Ant had the key to both homes, so he pulled out the key to unlock the door and they went inside. After looking around for about ten minutes, Pookie was satisfied. This is where he will start his new beginning.

Ant got so comfortable with Bonquisha that he started showing up unannounced more frequently. He was determined to get real close to her, so close that he could slide that ring right off her hand. Each time he showed up without calling first, he made sure he had a gift with him thinking that showering her with gifts would help his cause.

"You here agin'?!" Bonquisha asks with her head cocked to the side and her hand on her hip.

"I got these for you." he says and hands her a colorful bouquet of flowers with a big cheesy grin. Ant barges his way into her home. "Smells good in here. Whatchu' cookin'?" he asks.

"Uh, nuthin' fa you!" she responds while closing her door.

He makes himself comfortable on the couch. She is standing behind it looking at him like he has lost his ever-loving mind. Then he grabs the remote and starts to change the channel. This really infuriated Bonquisha as she was watching the news and he took it upon himself to change it to wrestling.

"Really? Wrestling?!" she asks, then proceeds to go back into the kitchen.

She was making some salmon and was trying to get that buttery sauce just right. Opening the freezer, she grabs another piece of salmon to add to the skillet. She wasn't the best cook but she was trying. Half hoping Ant would come into the kitchen and take over, she pretends to have a meltdown to get his attention.

"Oh no!" she says and peeks around the corner to see if he was coming.

"You okay in there?" he asks without taking his eyes off of the television.

"Oh, just in here messing up this salmon." she replies.

"Turn down your fire. You got it too high." he responds.

How he knew that without getting up was puzzling her. She did what he suggested and then joined him in the living room. This was attempt number two to get him to take over. He knew what she was trying to do and refused to give in until the last minute as he thought about his plan. When the commercial came on, he hopped up and went into the kitchen.

"Guhl, you got this stuff burning. Let me see if I can fix it." he says much to her liking.

"You are the cook!" she gives attitude and rolls her eyes. She knew what she was doing, and he did too.

After saving the meal, they sat down at the table to eat. He found the good stuff in the back of the cabinet and took it upon himself to serve it, much to her surprise. She gave him a scolding look but her anger didn't last long once she took one bite of the food. He knew the way to her heart was food because she loved to eat.

She didn't realize he had whipped up a dessert using a cake mix she had in the cabinet but thought she had smelled something sweet. He cleared the dishes from the table and went into the kitchen to retrieve the dessert. A huge smile came over her face because dessert was her thing! She absolutely loved dessert.

In the middle of eating the dessert, while she wasn't paying attention, Ant gets down on one knee. She looks up from her plate and sees what he is doing. Her eyes got big as he pulled out a small red box. As he begins to profess his love to her, he is slowly removing the ring Raheim gave her from her hand and placing the tiny one-half carat ring on her hand.

After quickly securing the ring that Raheim gave her in his pocket, he continues with the distraction by asking for her to be his woman. His heart is beating so fast that he hopes she doesn't hear or feel it. She is looking down at her hand and back at Ant's face. Thoughts were running through her mind and she was wondering what it would be like, is he for real, should she or shouldn't she. The last bite of dessert is calling her at the same time. She finishes it before answering.

They both stand up and as she is looking at her hand it is then that she realizes Ant was trying to rob her. She immediately went into her alter ego and pulled out all the rage in her. Jerking her hand out of his, she runs to get her purse. Ant knew what she was trying to do and immediately tripped her so that she fell before reaching it.

Fortunately, for her, she kept her phone in her back pocket. As she sat up on the floor, she slowly reached for the phone and was able to dial 9-1-1 before Ant knew what she was doing. The call went through before he took the phone from her and threw it across the room. He ties her up to prevent her from coming after him as he went into the bedroom to collect more of her valuables.

The operator from 9-1-1 had provided the necessary information to the police so that they could go and check out what might be occurring on the other end of the call. A police unit was in route but it would take some time for them to get there. Just how it was where she lived. Alexis had asked her to move in with her a long time ago and now she wished she had, however, that was no longer an option.

Little did Bonquisha know that one of KB's security detail team members was posted up nearby to keep an eye on her. He could hear on the police scanner that an officer was on the way and sent a message to KB about what he heard. After receiving instruction, he got out of the car and went to investigate the issue. KB was able to get a message to the officer that was in route and told him to turn off his sirens. Then he jumped into his car and drove to Bonquisha's.

Both the officer and KB got there at the same time as the officer decided to slow down and take his time getting there after receiving the message. KB made a mental note of the officer's actions to have addressed later. They connect with KB's security detail to get the scoop.

"Okay, you go around back." KB tells the police officer.

"You, come with me." he tells his security detail team member.

KB knocks on the door and then proceeds to kick in the door, with his security detail backing him. Bonquisha begins yelling that Ant is in the bedroom as the security detail begins to untie her. She is fuming, kicking, screaming, and crying, all at the same time.

KB proceeds to the bedroom. Just as he is in front of the door, Ant darts out and tries to run. In one move, KB takes him down. The security detail team member moves in to place the handcuffs on Ant. All of the jewelry he tried to steal fell all over the floor. The red box also rolled out of his pocket. He had placed Bonquisha's ring inside of it while grabbing her other jewelry in the bedroom.

Bonquisha runs over to where the red box landed and opens it. She sees the ring Raheim gave her and begins to cry. Looking up at KB, she mouths the words 'Thank you!'. Walking toward the couch she clutches the box close to her chest and tries to pull herself together.

Ant is in disbelief. He had no idea she was being watched. All he could think about is what Pookie was going to say and how could he let such greed get to him. As he is being escorted out of her home, Bonquisha pulls off the fake cubic zirconia ring and throws it at him. A few choice words followed as well.

BACK TOGETHER AGAIN

KB helped save Bonquisha. As a result, she had to back off of her plan to take him out, for now. Hopefully Pookie would be in agreement to stand down for a bit. All this time, she hadn't noticed KB's security detail was watching her but she was glad he was there. It was just as important for KB to keep an eye on her just as much as she was keeping an eye on Alexis, she figured.

After this ordeal, she was not going to let anyone ever get close to her again. For her safety, she decided to have a replica of the ring Raheim gave her made and store the original in a safe deposit box. First thing the next morning, that is exactly what she did. She also changed all of her locks and upgraded what she carried in her purse. The only good thing that came out of this was that she was able reconnect with Alexis. No more surveillance required. She was getting tired of that anyway.

About a week had passed since everything went down. Against KB's advice, Alexis loaded up Beautiful into her BMW X7 and drove over to Bonquisha's. KB turned on the tracker app on

Alexis' phone and connected to it as well. No more surprises, and he would also be able to track Bonquisha's every move.

As soon as Alexis left the driveway, Bonquisha's phone buzzed. She realized the tracker had been turned back on and that Alexis was heading her way. In the process of rushing to clean her house and make sure it was presentable, she stubs her toe on the corner of the couch. Shaking it off, she quickly prepares some refreshments. She couldn't contain her excitement that she was getting her friend back and she was hoping to spend time with Beautiful.

The doorbell rings and on the other side is Alexis with Beautiful in the baby carriage. Bonquisha opens the door and with outstretched arms she wraps them around Alexis who does the same. They are hugging and screaming and crying so loudly that Beautiful begins to cry. Not sure if she was scared or feeling left out, but she let them know either way.

"Oh baby, don't cry." Bonquisha looks down into the baby carriage and says to Beautiful. "She is so Beautiful! What a fitting name!" she says.

They enter her home and sit down on the couch. Bonquisha offers Alexis some lemonade and snacks. Conversation carries on as if they never spent any time apart. The bond was strong even though it had been some time.

"I can't believe you missed my wedding." Alexis says. "And the birth of Beautiful." she continues, not knowing Bonquisha hadn't missed either.

"I know! That was selfish of me. Fate brought us back together again. Did you receive the gift I left you?" Bonquisha says.

"Hmmm, I don't think I did. I will have to check when I get home. An' I know I saw you at the store that day. Were you following me?" Alexis asks. "I kept getting this strange feeling. That was you?" she inquires.

"Girl, you crazy!" Bonquisha replies, not really answering the questions. "Now hand over that baby!" she says.

Bonquisha is holding Beautiful and staring at her little cute face, her little cute hands, her little cute fingers. She is in awe and begins to tear up. Reaching for a tissue to wipe the tears before they fall, Alexis sees this and begins to tear up as well.

"Okay, Okay!! Let's get it together! We can't be doing all dis cryin'! We gotta be strong for Beautiful." Bonquisha commands.

They straighten up their act. Bonquisha hands Beautiful back over to Alexis who then gently rocks her to sleep. Placing her back into the baby carriage carefully so as not to wake her was always a challenge. For the first time, she did it with ease.

After another hour of conversation, Alexis notices the time and decides she should be getting home. She gets up to gather her things and gives her best friend a hug. Bonquisha walks her to her vehicle and helps her get Beautiful settled. One last hug and then Alexis gets in the driver's seat to start her journey home.

Bonquisha is thankful for the visit and watches Alexis drive off into the night. Praying she makes it home safely while continuing to watch her through the window. A combination of feelings come over her, happiness, anger, loneliness, sadness.

"We might be friends again, but this is far from over, far from over…"